PUFFIN B

WAYNE'S LUCK

Wayne just can't help causing chaos, even when he's doing something as simple as eating an ice-cream at the seaside. But then, that's brothers for you. And in the second story, Gemma is looking forward to going to a wedding for the first time, but then her mother says those dreadful words, 'Keep an eye on Wayne, Gemma,' and she knows she's in for trouble.

John Escott was born and brought up in Frome, Somerset, and has lived in Bournemouth for more than twenty years. He is married and has two children.

Also by John Escott

BURGLAR BELLS
RADIO ALERT
RADIO DETECTIVE
RADIO REPORTERS
RADIO RESCUE
A WALK DOWN THE PIER

Wayne's Luck

John Escott
Illustrated by Jacqui Thomas

PUFFIN BOOKS
in association with Blackie and Son Limited

PUFFIN BOOKS

Published by the Penguin Group
Penguin Books Ltd, 27 Wrights Lane, London W8 5TZ, England
Viking Penguin, a division of Penguin Books USA Inc,
375 Hudson Street, New York, New York 10014, USA
Penguin Books Australia Ltd, Ringwood, Victoria, Australia
Penguin Books Canada Ltd, 2801 John Street, Markham, Ontario, Canada L3R 1B4
Penguin Books (NZ) Ltd, 182–190 Wairau Road, Auckland 10, New Zealand

Penguin Books Ltd, Registered Offices: Harmondsworth, Middlesex, England

Wayne's Luck first published in Blackie Bears by Blackie and Son Limited 1989
Wayne's Wedding first published in Blackie Bears by Blackie and Son Limited 1988
Published in one volume in Puffin Books 1991
1 3 5 7 9 10 8 6 4 2

Printed in England by Clays Ltd, St Ives plc

Contents

Wayne's Luck

Wayne is a pain.

If you have a little brother, he can't be such a pain as Wayne.

'Keep an eye on Wayne,' Mum says. 'You know what he's like.'

Yes, I do. And certain people at Mura Sands know what he's like as well.

It was Dad's idea to go.

'Let's have a day at Mura Sands,' he said, looking out of the window at the first sunny day we'd had for ages.

'Where's Mura Sands?' Wayne asked. He had been there once but he'd been too small to remember it.

'It's by the sea,' I told him.

Dad found our old buckets and spades. Mum went off to get our bathing things and some towels. I made some squash in a plastic bottle. Wayne just got in everybody's way.

It took us an hour and a half to drive to Mura Sands. Wayne and I had Spotter sheets to keep us

from getting bored. In case you don't know, Spotter sheets are lists of things to look out for on the journey—rabbits, tractors, castles, fire stations—that sort of thing.

Mum writes out the lists before we leave and we tick things when we see them. At the end of the journey, we count up the ticks to see who spotted the most of anything.

Wayne cheats.

For instance, he did not see twenty-seven foxes between our house and Mura Sands. And how can you spot a lighthouse when you are still miles away from the sea?

Wayne just likes making ticks.

One thing that was not on our list was a sand artist. But Wayne spotted him almost as soon as we arrived.

'Look!' he yelled, peering out of the window as we sat in a traffic jam on the seafront.

'Look at what?' Dad said.

'Next to the pier,' Wayne said.

It was an old pier and it had an amusement arcade at the end.

'If I look round,' Dad said, 'we shall hit the car in front.'

'It's an old man,' I explained, 'and he's building models out of sand.'

The models were so real-looking, they made me shiver.

There was a tiger, a lion, a giraffe and a big fat polar bear. Behind them was a high sand wall which was the side of a ship, with portholes and an anchor. Round all this was a net, strung between poles.

'What's that net for?' asked Wayne.

'That's to protect the models,' said Dad.

The sand artist sat down in a deckchair. He had wispy white whiskers and a long thin face. He wore long shorts and his toes poked out of his sandals.

'The sand artist,' Mum said. 'I'd forgotten he was here.'

'Coo.' Wayne screwed up his

face, the way he always does
when something surprises him. A
man on the promenade thought
Wayne was being rude and shook
a fist at him.

I pretended I wasn't there.

Dad found a place to park and
we stopped off at a shop for some
salad rolls on the way to the
beach.

It was very crowded. We stepped over sandcastles, between deckchairs and dodged other kids racing in and out of the sea.

'Let's sit here,' Dad said, finding a space.

'I want to go in the sea!' cried Wayne. He pulled off all his clothes and dropped them on the sand.

'Go in with him, Gemma,' Mum said as Wayne put on his trunks. 'Keep an eye on him.'

That will be printed on my gravestone:

HERE LIES GEMMA
—SHE WORE HERSELF OUT KEEPING AN EYE ON HER BROTHER

The sea was cold but Wayne didn't notice. He swam and dived and pulled seaweed from the pebbly sea bed. He's like a fish in water. Dad says nobody really taught Wayne to swim, it just came naturally.

(Nobody taught him to be a pain either. That came naturally too.)

'I want a softee-whopper ice-cream,' he announced when we came out of the water.

Mum fished into her bag for a pound coin.

'Go and buy yourselves ice-creams then,' she said, giving the money to me. 'And come straight back.'

The ice-cream kiosk was just behind us on the promenade.

Wayne stepped backwards on to Mum's bag. Inside was the plastic bottle. It split down the middle with a crack and sticky lemon squash poured out over the salad rolls.

'I didn't see—' Wayne began.

'You didn't look!' I said.

18

'Get him out of here!' shouted
Dad.

We left them taking everything
out of Mum's bag.

There was a queue at the ice-
cream kiosk.

'I hate waiting in queues,' said
Wayne.

'Yes, well I can't help that, can
I?' I said.

19

'I could go and look at the sand models while you wait in the queue,' he said.

A little way along the beach, below the promenade, was the sand artist. A small crowd leaned against the railings, looking down at him.

'You're to stay with me,' I told Wayne.

'I'll be all right, Gemma,' he whined. 'I'll just go and stand there. I won't move and you'll be able to see me, anyway.'

I gave up. 'OK!' At least he wouldn't be there to nag me to buy him the biggest of the softee-whoppers, so that I'd be forced to have only a small one myself.

I bought the ice-creams and went to join Wayne. He was sitting down, his feet dangling over the sea wall, staring at the models.

'Here you are,' I said.

Wayne licked his ice-cream and a large blob stuck to the end of his nose. Wayne is disgusting when he eats ice-cream. I prefer not to watch.

That was why I didn't actually see the softee-whopper fall off the end of the cone and over the sea wall. I didn't actually see it land in the sand artist's lap as he sat in his deckchair.

But I heard his angry shout. 'Hey! What the—?'

The old man leapt out of his deckchair as ice-cream seeped through his shorts. He knocked the deckchair sideways against one of the poles which held up the net. Down went all the poles, and down went the net—on to the sand models!

People watched open-mouthed as animals crumbled into heaps or lost heads, legs and tails. The

sand artist struggled to get free of the net. He was shouting rude names at Wayne but Wayne didn't hear a word. He was howling because he'd lost his softee-whopper.

'Come on!' I shouted. I grabbed his arm and dragged him down to the beach. 'And don't say a word about this to Mum! She'll kill me. And then I'll kill you.'

Wayne just wailed louder.

By the time we got back he was only sniffing but Mum and Dad didn't notice because they were arguing.

'I thought you put it in the bag!' Dad snapped at Mum.

'And *I* thought I did!' Mum

shouted back. 'But it's your
wallet, after all.'

They scowled at one another.

'What's wrong?' I asked.

Mum sighed. 'Your father
can't find his wallet.'

'Your mother forgot to put it in
the bag,' Dad said.

'Does it matter?' I asked.

'Not if you don't mind walking home,' Dad growled. 'I shall need to put some petrol in the car to get us back and, as far as I know, they don't give it away free around here.'

Wayne began to whine again. 'I don't want to walk back. It's too far. I only have little legs—!'

'Shut up,' Dad said.

People around began to stare.

'There's ten pence change from the ice-creams,' I said.

'It's not enough, Gemma,' Mum said.

Wayne began to dig a hole. Sand flew everywhere.

'Do you mind, young man?' said a large, pink-faced lady in a peach-coloured sunsuit. She had just been showered in sand and it had stuck to the sun-tan cream on her arms and shoulders.

I went down to the water's edge.

There was a sudden shout and I looked towards Wayne, as I always do when there's any kind of fuss. The hole was now huge.

The trouble was, he'd dug it just behind the pink-faced lady's deckchair. The lady and the deckchair were now in Wayne's big hole. They had fallen in when the side of the hole had collapsed.

'Get me out!' the lady cried. Dad and Mum each held one of her arms and tried to pull her up. It wasn't easy.

I went back when things were sorted out.

'We'll have our lunch on the pier,' Mum said.

We walked along the shoreline. Mum and Dad walked behind Wayne and me. They were still trying to decide what to do. Dad

wanted to go to the police station,
to see if the police could help.

Wayne picked something up
and dropped it into his bucket.

'What's that?' I said.

'A crab,' Wayne said.

29

Sure enough, a crab about the size of Wayne's hand was moving sideways around the bottom of the bucket.

'What are you going to do with that?' I said.

'I'm going to take it home,' he said.

If we ever get home, I thought.

We walked up to the promenade and onto the pier, where we sat down and ate our sticky salad rolls. They tasted of lemon squash.

'I want to go in there,' said Wayne, when we'd finished. He pointed to the amusement arcade.

'We don't have enough money,' Dad said.

'Gemma's got the change from the ice-creams,' Wayne said.

Amazing what a good memory he's got when it suits him.

'Oh, all right,' Dad said. 'Go with him, Gemma. And stay where we can see you from here.'

Wayne grabbed his bucket.

'Why do you need that?' I asked.

'Crabby wants to go as well,' he said.

I hoped Crabby could stand the noise. It was deafening inside the arcade. Wayne pointed to a machine. 'I want a go on that,' he said. It was one where you put a two pence piece in the slot. The coin runs down a chute and joins a heap of others on a shelf. The shelf goes backwards and forwards, backwards and forwards, all the time. The coins on the edge look about to fall off any second. Sometimes, the one you put in knocks against the

others and some actually do fall over the edge.

They fall down on to another moving shelf with coins balancing on the edge. And if you're very lucky, which is hardly ever, some of these get knocked over the edge by the ones that came from the top. Get it?

Anyway, those two pence pieces empty into a little tray on the outside of the machine—and you've won them!

Usually there's about four pence.

'Let me have the change from the ice-creams,' Wayne said.

Such a nice polite boy, my brother.

'Here you are, but you'll need to change it into two pences.'

There was a little booth in the corner where a woman sat painting her nails and handing out change. A large dog with lots of long, untidy hair lay beside the booth. The woman and the dog looked rather alike.

'Two pence pieces, please,' Wayne said, putting the ten pence coin on the counter. As he did so, the dog sat up and sniffed at Wayne's bucket.

'Whisky!' growled the woman.

The dog slumped back onto the floor but it kept its eyes on the bucket as Wayne walked back and put it down next to the slot machine.

PLAYERS MUST NOT TILT, said a sign on the glass. It seemed a silly sign. Why did it matter whether a player leaned sideways or not?

Wayne fed in four coins, adding to the heap on the top shelf. Nothing happened.

'It doesn't work properly,' he grumbled.

He pushed the last coin into the slot and tried to kick the machine. He kicked his bucket instead. It rolled over and the crab scuttled out sideways, under the machine.

'Now look—' I began.

It was as far as I got. There was a sudden barking noise and a great rush of air as something went by me at top speed.

It was the dog with the long hair, barking its head off. It leapt against the side of the machine, trying to get at the crab. The machine rocked backwards and forwards as the dog banged against it. Two pence pieces began pouring out of the front in a great tidal wave. They fell into the tray and over Wayne's feet. He shrieked with delight and tried to catch them.

'I've won, I've won!' he yelled.

A large crowd gathered around us. Suddenly, a hand grabbed the

dog by its collar and dragged it off the machine. It was the woman from the booth.

'Whisky!' she shouted. 'Whisky, get down!'

It took some time to get the dog under control. Meanwhile, everybody was helping Wayne to pick up the two pence pieces and dropping them into his bucket.

'Well done, kid,' laughed a man with a beard. 'You've won the jackpot!'

The woman with the dog had other ideas. 'He can't have all that. He was cheating. The sign says no tilting the machine.'

'It was the dog who tilted the machine,' said the bearded man.

'Whose dog is it, anyway?'

The woman looked flustered.
'Well, it's mine but—'

'Then you should keep it under control,' said the man. He bent down and scooped up the last of the coins. 'Here, kid,' he said, dropping them into Wayne's bucket.

I grabbed Wayne's arm and we scooted.

We left the crab to look after itself.

Mum and Dad hadn't seen any
of this. When Wayne and I got
back, we discovered why. They
were busy talking to the pink-
faced lady who had fallen into
Wayne's hole. She was holding
Dad's wallet.

'Gemma,' Mum said, seeing
Wayne and me. 'This lady has
found Dad's wallet. Isn't it
wonderful?'

'I found it just after you left,' the lady said. 'Half buried in the sand where you were sitting.'

'It must have fallen there when we emptied out your bag,' Dad said to Mum. 'After Wayne stood on the lemon squash bottle.'

They were all smiling like old friends now. Pity about the police station, I thought, but at least we would get home.

'. . . and we're sorry about that hole,' Dad was saying.

The lady forced a little laugh. 'Never mind,' she said, glancing at Wayne. 'I'm sure he's not usually any trouble to anyone.'

It was then that Wayne hid his bucket of money behind him.

He kept it hidden all the way
along the pier as we headed back
to the car, Mum and Dad in front
of us.

'What will you do with the
money?' I whispered.

'I don't know,' Wayne said. You could tell he didn't really want it now. Money meant nothing to Wayne. Winning things was what he enjoyed. But this prize would have to be explained to Mum and Dad sometime.

'You didn't really win it, you know,' I said. 'The dog did.'

Wayne scowled and said nothing, which meant he agreed with me but wasn't going to say so.

'You don't actually deserve it,' I went on.

'Well, I couldn't give it to the dog, could I?' he said. 'And that woman was horrible. I wasn't going to let her have it.'

We were on the promenade now, threading our way through the crowds. Wayne began to hurry and I realized he was anxious to get past the sand artist.

It was then I had the idea. I think it's the best idea I've ever had.

'Quick,' I said to Wayne. 'Give me your bucket.'

He stared at me but handed it over. I pushed through the crowd to the railings.

Below, the sand artist was still repairing his models, although most of them looked quite healthy again. Directly below me was his hat where people dropped their coins.

I held Wayne's bucket over it.
Wayne gave a little cry from
behind me but I ignored it.
Instead, I emptied all the money
into the sand artist's hat.

The old man's mouth fell open in surprise. He began to say something—something nice I think—but I didn't wait to hear it. I grabbed Wayne and ran after Mum and Dad before they could begin wondering where we were.

After all, I was supposed to be keeping an eye on Wayne, wasn't I?

Wayne's Wedding

Wayne is my brother. He is five
years old and I am nearly seven.

'Keep an eye on Wayne,
Gemma,' Mum is always
saying. 'You know what he's
like.'

I do know what he's like.
Everybody knows what Wayne
is like. If they don't, they should
have come to THE WEDDING

and then they would have found
out.

It's funny but I always think
of THE WEDDING in big
letters. It must be because of all
the things that happened.

I'll tell you about them...

It was a Saturday morning.
We were all having breakfast
when Mum broke the news.

'Patsy Millar is getting
married next Saturday,' she
said. 'We are all going to the
wedding.'

Wayne made a face.

'Weddings are boring,' he
said.

'You've never been to one

before, so how do you know?' I
said.

Wayne didn't answer. He just
screwed up his nose. He was
probably thinking of Patsy
Millar. She was the daughter of
Dad's boss, Mr Millar. She was
tall and skinny with huge teeth.

'Anyway,' said Mum. 'You have to come to the wedding, and that's that. Gran will be away that day and there's nobody else to look after you. Gemma will keep an eye on you.'

Mum said this in her don't-you-dare-argue voice.

It was the first wedding I had been to. In fact, I'd begun to think nobody was ever going to invite me to one and that I wouldn't know what to do at my own.

Wayne hates going anywhere if it means dressing up. He hates it only slightly less than having his hair washed.

'I feel like a Christmas parcel!' he wailed the following Saturday morning. Mum had forced him to dress in itchy-new trousers, squeaky-new shoes, a pink shirt and a pink tie.

I had a new strawberry coloured dress and shoes. Mum looked at both of us and nodded.

'You'll do,' she said.

Wayne had kicked up such a fuss about being made tidy, we were late getting to the church. He always makes us late getting to places. It makes me mad!

The Vicar was in the church porch waiting for Patsy Millar to arrive.

'I'm so sorry we're late,' Mum said, as she and I ran up the church steps.

Dad was still pulling Wayne out of the car.

'The bride is late as well,' said the Vicar, 'so you're all right.'

'I want to sit in the front row,' Wayne said when Dad dragged him to the church door.

'You can't,' Dad said. 'That's

for the bride's family. We shall sit at the back.'

'But I shan't be able to see what happens!' Wayne cried.

'You didn't want to come anyway,' I reminded him.

He just scowled at me.

The Vicar tried to put things right. 'How would you like to sit next to my wife?' he said. 'She plays the organ. You'll be able to see everything from up there.'

'Go with him, Gemma,' Mum said, as Wayne rushed off down the aisle before anybody could argue. 'Keep an eye on him.'

How many eyes was I supposed to have, I wondered as I hurried after Wayne.

The church was full. Ladies
wearing large hats gave us
peculiar looks as we trotted
towards the organ at the side of
the altar.

'Hallo,' said the Vicar's wife, smiling. She didn't seem to mind having company.

Not at first, anyway.

Not until Wayne slipped off the organ stool and put his feet on the pedals.

BLAAAAGH! went the organ,

just as Patsy Millar, looking much prettier than I remembered her, reached the altar.

Patsy gave a little scream and dropped her flowers.

'Sorry!' Wayne shouted across to her as he scrambled back up on to the stool with a couple more BLAAAGH-BLAAAGHs!

'Shut up!' I hissed at him.

After that, the Vicar's wife made several mistakes. Just having Wayne near seemed to make her nervous. He does that to people, I've noticed.

After the service, the photographer took pictures of the bride and bridegroom outside the church. Then he took pictures of some of the guests. Wayne ran around after the photographer and got into four of the pictures before I spotted him and dragged him away.

'They don't want you to remind them of their wedding day,' I told him. 'Although after that terrible noise you made on the organ, they're not likely to forget you.'

'I just slipped,' Wayne said. 'After that, the organ lady played lots of wrong notes.'

'You're enough to make anyone play wrong notes!' I said.

Soon Dad and Mum came over. 'Come on,' Dad said. 'Let's drive to the reception.'

'Reception?' Wayne said. 'What's that?'

'The eating and drinking bit,' Dad said.

'Oh,' Wayne said, smiling. 'That sounds better.'

The wedding reception was at the biggest and poshest hotel in the town. Wayne went round five times in the revolving door before Dad yanked him inside.

We went into a small room
where the wedding presents were
spread out on a huge table.

'Where's the food?' Wayne
asked.

'Shh!' I said. 'Just wait, will you? Look at the lovely presents.'

Wayne stared at an ugly-looking cuckoo clock.

'I hope nobody gives me one of those when I get married,' he said in a loud voice.

Several people looked at Wayne as if he was something nasty that had crawled out from under the skirting board.

The meal was served in a much larger room with a stage at one end. We all sat down and had a chicken salad and some sort of gooey pink mixture afterwards. And a piece of wedding cake so small that Wayne asked a waitress for another slice.

'You can't have any more,' I whispered to him. 'Everybody gets just one piece.'

But, would you believe it, the waitress brought him some more! Then she disappeared

before I had a chance to ask for
another slice.

The speeches came next. The
bride's father began by saying
what a wonderful girl Patsy was
and how he would miss her.

I stared out of the window. There was a swimming pool in the garden of the hotel. It was shaped like a heart and the blue water shone in the sun. Sunbeds and deckchairs were spread about the lawn but nobody was around.

I closed my eyes and imagined myself jumping into the lovely cool, blue water. Away from the stuffy room and the boring voices.

When I opened my eyes, Wayne was no longer sitting beside me.

I looked up and down the room.

At the stage.

Under the table.

No Wayne.

Mum and Dad were so busy listening to the speeches, they didn't notice that Wayne had disappeared.

I looked out into the garden again.

And saw Wayne taking off all his clothes.

His itchy-new trousers, his squeaky-new shoes, his pink tie, his pink shirt, his pants and socks.

Then he walked down into the blue swimming pool!

Wayne loves swimming. He goes to the baths each week and doesn't need arm bands or a rubber ring.

I watched him now, floating on his back, splashing his feet up and down. He was having a very good time.

But I had to do something. And quickly, before somebody noticed him. Otherwise I'd be in

trouble. 'Keep an eye on him,'
Mum had said.

Getting up very quietly, I
crept out through an open patio
door and ran down towards the
pool.

'Wayne!' I called.

Wayne didn't seem to hear.

Or he pretended not to.

'Wayne!' I called again.

'Shall I fetch a towel, miss?' said a voice from behind me.

It was a hotel waitress. The one who had given Wayne the extra slice of wedding cake.

'Er—thank you. He's—er—my brother,' I explained.

The waitress smiled. 'He seems to be enjoying himself,' she said. Then she went to fetch the towel.

Enjoying himself! 'Wayne!' I yelled. 'Get out of that pool at once!'

Wayne blew bubbles across the water. He didn't look surprised to see me.

'You should come in too,

Gemma,' he said. 'It's lovely.'

The waitress arrived back
with a huge fluffy white towel.
The name of the hotel was
printed on one side. It looked
big enough for two Waynes. She
handed it to me, trying not to
laugh, and then went away.

'Come on in, Gem,' Wayne
shouted.

I whirled round. 'You come OUT!' I told him, in a voice that sounded so much like Mum's it startled me.

And it worked.

'Oh, all right,' Wayne grumbled, and he walked up out of the water on to the blue tiles around the pool.

He was looking over my shoulder at something. I turned to see what it was.

Mum's shocked face stared through the window. Her nose was pressed against the glass. She looked as if she had seen a ghost.

There were other noses pressed against the glass as well.

Wayne smiled and gave them all a wave before taking the fluffy white towel.

'Wayne!' Mum burst out of the door and ran towards the pool. 'Gemma! What on earth...?'

'I've had a lovely swim,' Wayne said, wiping himself dry.

I was opening and shutting my mouth, trying to think of something to say.

'Swim indeed!' Mum was furious. She snatched the towel and bundled Wayne into his clothes. 'Why didn't you keep an eye on him, Gemma? I've never been so embarrassed in all my life. What will all those people think? What will Mr Millar think? What—?'

Then an awful thing happened.

Mum stepped back on to some wet tiles beside the pool and slipped. 'Aaagh!' she cried, as she fell into the water with a huge SPLASH!

I closed my eyes. It's something I often do when trouble is on the way. When I opened them again, we were in the middle of a crowd. All the other guests had come into the garden. Dad had rolled up his trousers and was wading out towards Mum.

Suddenly, Mrs Millar, the bride's mother, grabbed Wayne by the arm and started to drag him towards the hotel. 'Come with me!' she shrieked. 'You too, Gemma.'

I followed. It seemed the best thing to do. Anyway, I didn't want to be around when Mum came out of the water.

Mrs Millar stamped along the hallway and opened a door. It was the room where all the wedding presents were spread out.

'Wait in here,' she told us. 'And DON'T TOUCH ANYTHING.' Her face was red and she looked as if she wanted to strangle Wayne. Well, she will have to join a queue, I thought.

CUCKOO! went the ugly cuckoo clock as Mrs Millar left the room.

I gave a big sigh. 'What a wedding this is turning out to be,' I said.

'What's the matter?' Wayne said, looking all innocent. 'I'm enjoying it.'

'It's all right for you,' I said. 'Mum and Dad will go mad when we get home and I'll get ticked off. It isn't fair.'

Wayne stared at the wedding presents, screwing up his nose. The table was covered with a large white tablecloth which hung over the front, reaching to the floor.

A smile spread slowly across Wayne's face. Then, quick as a flash, he ducked down and crawled under the table.

'Wayne, come out,' I said in my stern voice.

He didn't come out.

'Stop messing about and come out!' I said in a louder voice.

A lump appeared in the tablecloth and I could hear Wayne snorting with laughter.

'I'll come and get you,' I threatened.

More snorting.

'Right then.' I dropped onto my hands and knees and dived into the darkness beneath the tablecloth.

As I did so, somebody came into the room.

We both knelt there and held our breath. Then I lifted the edge of the tablecloth.

A pair of legs in green trousers stood very close to my nose.

The next thing we heard was something being taken from the table top. Were they packing up the presents ready to go? If so, the tablecloth would be whisked off very soon.

Then the green-trousered legs moved away.

Quickly.

And on tiptoe.

Something was wrong, I knew

it was. I lifted the cloth a teeny
bit higher—and my heart
jumped!

A hotel porter in his green
uniform had the cuckoo clock
under one arm. He was peering
into the hall to see if anybody
was about.

He's stealing it! The words screamed silently inside my head and I dropped the tablecloth to the floor again.

'What's happening?' Wayne asked in a low voice.

I told him in a whisper.

'A THIEF!' he yelled and, without thinking, he stood up and banged his head. 'OW!'

He tried to get out from under the table and became hopelessly tangled up in the white cloth.

It must have frightened the porter half to death, which was hardly surprising. All the man saw was a white tablecloth with a pair of moving bumps under it. And all he heard were

Wayne's blood-curdling howls
as he rubbed his sore head.

Anyway, the porter dropped
the cuckoo clock as if it was a
lump of hot coal.

COOO-CUCK! COOO-
CUCK! COOO-CUCK!

I peered out from under the tablecloth in time to see a small bird bursting out of the front of the clock and some important looking springs falling out of the back. COOO-CUCK! COOO-CUCK! COOO-CUCK! On and on went the noise. The clock seemed to have gone crazy.

People ran in to see what was happening. One of them was the Hotel Manager.

He saw a white-faced porter pressed against the door frame, watching the ghostly, moving tablecloth where Wayne was still trying to get out. He also saw the cuckoo clock and quickly realized what had happened.

'Why, you thieving—!'

The rest of the Manager's
words were drowned in an even
louder COOOOOO-CUCK!
before the clock shuddered into
silence.

Wayne and I crawled out
from under the table.

'What's happening now?' Mrs Millar wailed.

'I think these two young people have stopped a thief stealing your daughter's wedding presents,' the Hotel Manager told her. He put a firm hand on the porter's arm.

Mum and Dad were at the front of the crowd, their mouths open like trap doors. Mum's dress was making a puddle of water around her feet.

'Well done, you two,' the Hotel Manager went on, smiling at Wayne and me. 'Who knows what else this thief might have taken if you hadn't been clever enough to frighten him.'

Wayne grinned and looked
pleased with himself.

I just felt sick.

'Er—I think it's time we went
home,' Dad said, stepping
forward and taking hold of
Wayne's hand.

'Oh, must you go?' said the
Manager.

'Yes, we must,' Dad said.

93

'Definitely,' Mum said, dripping into her puddle.

While we were driving home in the car, I decided I probably wouldn't get married when I grew up. At least, if I did, I would not have a big wedding.

Or if I did have a big wedding, I would NOT invite my brother Wayne.

After all, who would keep an eye on him?

Would you?